Did you know that word-for-word, professional audio support for this book is available at Book Buddy?

GoReader™ powered by Book Buddy is pre-loaded with word-for-word audio support to build strong readers and achieve Common Core standards.

The corresponding GoReader™ for this book can be found at: http://bookbuddyaudio.com

Or send an email to: info@bookbuddyaudio.com

SHOOTOUT

A MAGIC LOCKER ADVENTURE

PETE BIRLE

Shootout
A Magic Locker Adventure

Scobre Educational
2255 Calle Clara
La Jolla, CA 92037

Scobre Operations & Administration
42982 Osgood Road
Fremont, CA 94539

www.scobre.com
info@scobre.com

Scobre Educational publications may be purchased for educational, business, or sales promotional use.

Cover and layout design by Jana Ramsay
Copyedited by Renae Reed

ISBN: 978-1-62920-125-2 (Soft Cover)
ISBN: 978-1-62920-124-5 (Library Bound)
ISBN: 978-1-62920-123-8 (eBook)

TABLE OF CONTENTS

1
THE SWAMPS OF JERSEY

"Super Bowl?" asked Juanito. "It looks like we're in the middle of nowhere."

As far as the eye could see, there were weeds—cattails, to be exact. The kids didn't know it, but they were looking out at the salt marsh of the New Jersey Meadowlands.

But they were standing on concrete.

"Where are we?" Jamie asked, now standing next to her friends.

"Look *this* way," said MJ, who was staring in the

opposite direction.

Jamie and Juanito spun around to see what MJ was looking at.

"Oh my!" said Jamie, her eyes as wide as beach balls.

"Oh yes!" said Juanito. "Giants Stadium!"

The three youngsters stood and stared at the huge football stadium located in the swamps of North Jersey. Although what they were looking at had since been knocked down and replaced by the even more colossal MetLife Stadium, they were in awe at its size.

"There must be a game going on," MJ finally said. "Look at all those people heading into the stadium."

"Well, it's not the Super Bowl," said Jamie. "Everyone is in shorts. It's summertime."

The kids were standing at the far edge of one of the parking lots, out of sight of the fans. At that moment, men, women, and children of all ages were pouring in by the busload. Within minutes, a hundred cars would be looking to park exactly where they were standing.

"We better move the locker," said Jamie. "Whatever's going on here today is a sellout."

The kids pushed the locker up over the curb and into the cattails. Then, they started following the crowd toward the stadium.

As they walked, a man selling T-shirts approached them. He asked if they were interested in buying one.

"What's it say?" asked MJ.

The man held up a shirt with various countries' flags on it. Below the flags were the words "FIFA Women's World Cup, USA, 1999."

2
TROUBLE FOR DENMARK

"Don't you see what's happening?" Jamie asked her friends as they walked toward the stadium.

"What do you mean?" asked MJ.

"We're helping athletes in *all* of the sports we played on report card day," said Jamie. "First hockey, then baseball, football, and now soccer."

"Alright!" exclaimed MJ. He even surprised himself with how excited he sounded.

"A while ago, you couldn't wait to get home," said Juanito. "Now, you can't get enough time travel."

The three of them broke into laughter upon that comment. Within minutes, the kids had made it across the parking lot to just outside one of the stadium gates when Jamie's eyes lit up. "I'd bet my allowance we're here to help the U.S. women's soccer team win the World Cup," she said.

"I don't see how we're going to be able to do that this afternoon," said MJ. "We don't have tickets."

"We're sunk," said Juanito.

"Don't be so sure," said the Coach, at that moment arriving to walk alongside them.

The crowd had grown even larger by that time. It seemed like everyone on the East Coast had come to cheer on the U.S. women in the worldwide soccer tournament that is held every four years.

There were groups of people coming from all directions, trying to make their way through the gate. There was a lot of pushing and shoving, and things started to get a bit dangerous. The kids noticed a group of people arguing near the entrance. They were shouting. Then, a fight broke out. Within seconds, though, security was on the scene to quickly restore order.

A few minutes later, several security guards led three young men away. The children overheard one of the guards say that, for starting the commotion, the men would not be able to see the game. As they brushed past the kids, an envelope fell out of one of the guys' pockets. Juanito bent down to pick it up. Inside were three tickets to that day's game, June 19, 1999.

He held them up for the others to see.

"Well, at least we know we're going to see *this* game," said Jamie, taking the tickets out of Juanito's hand. She smiled, then looked over to the Coach to thank him. But he was already gone.

"More magic," said Juanito. "Way cool."

"Who's playing?" asked MJ.

"Denmark and the United States," said Jamie.

"What do you think we're supposed to do?" asked Juanito.

"Let's find out," said MJ, grabbing one of the tickets out of Jamie's hand. "I wonder if we've got good seats."

After handing their tickets to one of the stadium employees, the boys and Jamie made their way in.

"Is Denmark that good?" asked Jamie, looking around. "I can't believe how many people are here!"

The Coach returned at that moment, walking alongside her.

"There are nearly 80,000 people here today, for the *first* game," he said. "Isn't that something? And games that don't include the Americans are selling out all over the country," he added.

"I didn't know girls' soccer was that popular," said MJ.

"Women's soccer, son," said the Coach. "It's getting there. Not only is the U.S. team expected to win, but a victory by the Americans will help make the case for the start-up of a women's professional league.

"This is a defining moment for the sport," he

continued. "In many ways, the sport in the United States depends on the American team's success."

The Coach stopped to let about a dozen 14-year-old girls go up the escalator ahead of him. It was obviously a soccer team.

"So I guess our women's team was pretty good in '99," Juanito said, watching what seemed like hundreds of girls' soccer teams go up the stadium steps.

"I'll say," answered the Coach. "They won the first women's world championship in 1991 and the Olympic gold medal in 1996."

"So this was their World Cup to lose, huh?" pondered MJ.

"You could say that," responded the Coach.

A few minutes later, the kids had reached their seats. They realized they were sitting in the first row of Section 111, on the field level, right behind the U.S. bench.

They gave each other high fives.

"Oh man!" giggled Juanito. "We're *so* close."

"I wonder if we'll be able to meet any players," said MJ.

"I wonder if we're going to find out why we're here *right now*," said Jamie, turning to find that the Coach was no longer with them. The kids all sighed at once. It was just like the Coach to leave, so they could experience the locker's magic on their own.

At that moment, the goalkeeper for the Americans came running over behind the United States' bench. She began frantically looking for something on the ground. After a few seconds, she abruptly stopped rummaging around the bench and approached the kids.

"Did any of you see a pair of goalie gloves?" she asked excitedly.

"We just got here," said MJ.

"You're Briana Scurry, aren't you?" asked Jamie, who really did know her famous athletes. "They call you 'The Rock,' right?"

"Yup," said Scurry. "Only, I won't be much of one

today if I don't find my lucky gloves."

"You lost your goalie gloves?" asked Juanito.

"Appears so," replied Scurry. "I woke up in the middle of the night and just knew something was wrong. Great timing, huh? Our first game in the World Cup is about to start."

"Where do you think you lost them?" asked Jamie, genuinely concerned.

"I don't know," she said. "I thought I brought them with me."

"Do you have a backup pair?" asked MJ.

"Yes, of course," said Scurry. "But I was hoping to wear my lucky gloves."

"We'll find them for you," blurted Jamie. The sentence was out of her mouth before she even realized what she had said. She turned to give her friends an encouraging look. "Right, guys?"

"Uh, yeah," stammered MJ. "We'll see if we can find them for you."

"Thanks, kid," said Scurry with a chuckle. The look

on her face told the children she didn't really think they could help, but she was willing to play along—just to be nice.

"You know, the pressure is really on us," she said. "We're not supposed to lose."

Just then, the best goalkeeper in the world grabbed her backup pair of gloves out of a duffel bag. Before returning to the field, she said, "Do I know you three from somewhere? You look familiar."

"I don't think so," said Jamie. "We've never met."

"If you say so," said Briana. "I could swear I've seen you guys somewhere." She turned and jogged away.

"That was weird," said Juanito.

"Yeah," said MJ. "We're from the future. How could we have met her?"

They settled into their seats.

"I can't believe she lost her gloves," said Juanito.

"I can't believe we just met Briana Scurry," said Jamie.

"I can't believe you told her we'll find her gloves," said MJ, turning to Jamie. "We don't know if that's how we're supposed to help."

"Do you think it's by chance?" asked Jamie. "Gee, boys can be so dumb sometimes. I mean, it's obvious: We're supposed to find Briana Scurry's lucky goalie gloves—and *before* the championship game in three weeks."

The boys looked at each other and nodded. It *was* kind of obvious. The locker transports them to the 1999 Women's World Cup, where three tickets to the U.S. team's first game fall into their hands. Then, they meet goalkeeper Briana Scurry and learn of her problem.

"So, should we leave now and start looking for the gloves?" asked Juanito.

"I don't see how we'll be able to find them in time for this game," said Jamie. "We might as well stay and watch."

The three kids sat back to watch the Danish team take it to the Americans right from the start. With just two minutes gone, Denmark fired a shot at Scurry, but it was wide of the left post. A few minutes later, Scurry made a great save of a header off a corner kick.

Scurry's save was just what the U.S. team needed to get going. Defender Brandi Chastain fed the ball to forward Mia Hamm on the right side. Hamm proceeded to slam it in the goal for a 1-0 U.S. lead.

The American defense took command from that point forward. Two insurance goals by Julie Foudy and Kristine Lilly sealed the victory for the United States.

After the game, the kids watched as U.S. Coach Tony DiCicco and Scurry were being interviewed by a television reporter right in front of them.

"Bri never looks panicked," the coach said. "She always looks calm, even when she isn't. That's key for a goalkeeper."

The reporter turned his microphone on Scurry.

"When my team is down in the other end, I love it," they heard her say. "It's fine with me if we're dominating. The more bored I am, the better."

But Jamie, MJ, and Juanito wondered if she would have felt even *better* had she been wearing her lucky gloves . . . especially since she had more World Cup games to play.

3
AN ALL-AROUND ATHLETE

Following the game, the three friends made their way back to the parking lot. They found the locker hidden in the weeds and got inside. The door closed behind them.

Within seconds, it swung open.

"Now, where are we?" asked Jamie, as she poked her head outside.

"Anoka," said MJ, reading the words on the building in front of him. They said "Anoka High School."

"Where's Anoka?" asked Juanito, scrunching his

face up so that it looked like a big question mark.

"I have no idea," said MJ. "But we better hide the locker—there are a bunch of kids coming this way."

Just as a group of high school students turned the corner, the youngsters pushed the locker into some bushes and out of sight.

"I'll ask those guys and girls about Anoka High School," said Juanito. "Maybe they can help us.

"Anoka High School," he said, approaching the students and trying to sound much older than he was. "I can't wait till I can go here."

"Best high school in Minnesota, kid," said a tall, muscular boy wearing a varsity football jacket. He patted Juanito on the head as he and his friends shuffled on by.

Jamie and MJ looked at each other. They were in Anoka, *Minnesota*. But why?

"Hey, where are you guys headed?" asked Juanito, determined to find out more information.

"To the soccer field," said a girl. "Isn't that why

you're here? To watch the Tornadoes win the state championship? That's why everyone is here."

That's when the kids noticed the crowd, off to the right, making its way toward the field. Apparently, there was a big soccer game going on.

"Oh yeah, the game," said Juanito. "Of course. . . . We just didn't know where the field was."

"Follow us," said the boy.

Jamie and MJ joined Juanito as they walked behind the teens.

"Man, it's cold here," said Jamie, wrapping her arms around her shoulders.

"It's Minnesota," said MJ. "It's supposed to be cold."

Just then, the kids spotted the field, where the Anoka High School girls' soccer team was warming up. They immediately noticed the girl knocking away practice shots in front of the Tornadoes' net. It was Briana Scurry, although a much younger version than the one they had met in New Jersey.

"We've gone back even further in time," said Jamie. "I wonder what year Briana Scurry played high school soccer."

She didn't have to wait long for the answer. A voice came over the loudspeaker.

"Ladies and gentlemen, welcome to the first round of the 1989 Minnesota girls' soccer state championship."

"1989!" said MJ. "We just went back another 10 years."

The three found a spot in the bleachers and sat down, just as the game began. They all kept their eyes glued to the Tornadoes' goalie, Briana Scurry.

She was a joy to watch. Although still developing, Scurry was a star at her position. She always kept her eyes on the ball, anticipating what would happen next. She knew when to stay on her line and when to come out. Once she did, she was skillful at cutting down the angle to the goal as she barked out instructions to her defenders.

And then, when it became necessary, she would leap into the air or dive along the ground to block a shot.

"It's no wonder she becomes the goalkeeper for the U.S. national team," said Juanito. "She was super in high school."

"Shh, keep your voice down," whispered Jamie. "We don't want anyone to know we've come here from the future."

"That's good advice, Jamie," said the Coach, who reappeared next to them in the bleachers. "Remember, only I am invisible."

For the rest of the game, the children asked the Coach questions about Briana Scurry.

They learned that Briana came from the only African-American family in her town of Dayton, a small farming community just up Route 10 from Anoka. They learned that she was one of only a handful of black kids in her high school, too.

And they learned that she excelled at whatever sport

she played. She was apparently great at basketball, softball, and track. She was even a wiz at karate.

"Basketball has helped with her footwork and speed, running track has given her endurance, and softball and karate have helped her hand-eye coordination and quickness," said the Coach. "Playing goalie just allows her to use all those skills at once."

"Are the goalie gloves she's wearing today her favorite pair?" Juanito asked the Coach.

"Perhaps," he answered. "But she's played without gloves. Personally, I don't think she even needs them."

They continued to watch Anoka's acrobatic goalkeeper make save after save. By the time the Tornadoes had disposed of their opponent, Scurry had turned in yet another all-star performance.

As they got up to leave, a nearby fan offered some predictions:

"I bet Anoka goes on to win the state championship. And I bet Briana will be named an All-American and the top female athlete in Minnesota. You just wait and see."

Juanito turned to ask the Coach whether these things would indeed happen, but the old man was once again gone.

"Do you think we should be looking to grab the goalie gloves Briana is wearing?" he asked Jamie instead.

"Or another pair she might have here in Minnesota?" asked MJ.

"I don't think the gloves Briana Scurry is looking for at the '99 World Cup are here, 10 years earlier," said Jamie. "Gloves she wore in high school probably wouldn't fit her hands anymore. Plus, they'd most likely be too beat up to use. . . .

"Something tells me we've got at least one more trip ahead of us."

They raced each other to the locker.

4
ONE SNEAKS BY

Upon opening the door, the kids realized that they had left Minnesota. Only, they hadn't returned to the Meadowlands.

They were in Chicago, in the locker room at Soldier Field. It was June 24, 1999. The United States was about to square off against Nigeria, in the second game of group play for both teams.

Seeing no real need to hide the locker this time, the kids made their way to the field. In the tunnel along the way, they picked up three field passes that, once again, magically were on the ground in front of them. They hung the passes around their necks and headed for the sunlight.

Emerging from inside the stadium, they found more than 65,000 screaming fans—and Briana Scurry, stretching on the sideline.

"Hey, it's you guys!" called the goalkeeper when she saw the children. "You three sure get around."

The kids smiled awkwardly.

"Any luck finding your gloves?" asked MJ.

"I was just going to ask you the same thing," said Scurry. "I was hoping you came down here to give me the good news."

"No, we haven't found them yet," said Jamie. "But we're on the case."

"Good," said Scurry. "The competition is only going to get tougher for us, and I'm hoping I can get my lucky gloves on my hands in time."

At that, she winked and ran onto the field. Over her shoulder, she yelled back, "But I still think I know you guys from somewhere."

Jamie, MJ, and Juanito shrugged at each other, then watched Briana Scurry, with her backup goalie gloves, attempt to stop Nigeria.

The Africans came out aggressively to start the game, launching an all-out attack. Using their quickness, they beat the Americans to the ball. Before the game was two minutes old, Nigeria's top player, "Marvelous" Mercy Akide, took advantage of a misplayed header to find an open teammate. Out of position, Scurry had no choice but to watch the perfectly placed shot find the back of the net for a 1-0 Nigerian lead.

The youngsters looked at each other with fear in their eyes.

They did it again moments later, when two U.S. defenders collided. Scurry would once again be put to the test. Forced to come off her line, she challenged for the loose ball. As a result, the Nigerians rushed their shot, which went past the post and over the end line.

The missed opportunity seemed to frustrate the Africans, while it sparked the Americans. The United States scored three times in less than three minutes of play and then finished even stronger, winning in a romp, 7-1.

Despite the shaky start, the Americans were virtually a lock to be in the quarterfinals.

"Now what?" asked Juanito.

"We see where the locker takes us next," said Jamie. "Don't let the final score fool you. Scurry let up a goal. That's not like her. We better get busy looking for those gloves."

5
MINUTEWOMAN

It was warm and muggy. And everywhere you looked, it was maroon.

The kids had traveled to the campus of the University of Massachusetts in Amherst, where they were just now hiding their locker in the woods.

They were next to the home field of the UMass Minutewomen. A group of female soccer players were engaged in a springtime pickup game. A familiar face was in one goal. It was Briana Scurry.

"We've gone back again," said Jamie.

"Yup," said MJ. "We're now going to see Briana Scurry as she was in college."

"Not only that, we're going to get a chance to play with her," said Juanito. "Look!"

The women on the field were motioning for the three time travelers to join them.

"Hey kids," yelled Scurry from in front of the goal. "We need a few more players. Want to join us?"

"You bet we do!" called Jamie.

"And I bet we've got soccer gear in the locker," said MJ. "Let's go check."

After motioning to Scurry and her teammates to wait a moment, the kids ran back to the locker to find cleats and a full soccer kit for each of them: shirts, shorts, socks, and shin guards.

As they changed into their "uniforms," the light bulb went off over Jamie's head again.

"Hey guys," she said. "Now we know why Briana Scurry thinks she remembers us in 1999. She does—we played soccer with her when she was in college."

MJ and Juanito stopped to let it soak in. This time travel was indeed the trip of a lifetime.

A few minutes later, they were on the field, showing off their talents. Once again, the locker had given them super athletic skills. There was one play in particular:

It started with MJ. He trapped a pass on his chest, directed the ball down to his feet, and proceeded to dribble past two Minutewomen like a world-class offensive player. Spotting Jamie making a run to the outside, he hit her with a perfect pass.

Jamie received the ball and turned, herself beating not one, but two opponents with some nifty foot skills. Then, she took off for the right corner. No one could match her speed. As she approached the end line, she launched a beautiful cross into the box.

Despite being the smallest player on the pitch by several feet, Juanito wormed his way between a pair of defenders, establishing position. As the ball came down, he went up. With what appeared to be rockets in his cleats, Juanito out-jumped everyone to head it past

Scurry into the far corner of the net.

"Wow," was all "the Rock"—not to mention the rest of her teammates—could say.

It was the kids' moment to shine, because after that goal, the 5-foot, 9-inch Scurry was perfect guarding her net. At 24 feet wide and 8 feet high, the goal made her look even smaller. But she didn't let anything else get by her.

She was so quick that she hardly ever dove. At the end of the game, Jamie explained to her friends what a huge advantage this was: By staying on her feet, Scurry had a better chance of stopping rebounds than if she were lying on the ground.

"You kids talking about Briana Scurry? She's something, huh?" said a man with a distinctive New England accent. "I got to see her play here for four years."

"Was she good?" asked Juanito, already knowing the answer.

"Good? She was wicked great!" said the man.

"Before she even got here, she was a high school All-American who was voted the top athlete in Minnesota her senior year."

The three friends from the future glanced at each other. The Anoka fan's predictions had indeed come true.

"Then, once here, she got even better. Quick as a panther and just as fearless," said the man. "She will graduate in a few days as a collegiate All-American who won college soccer's Goalkeeper of the Year award."

"How do you know so much about her?" asked MJ.

"I had the privilege of coaching her. I'm Jim Rudy," he said.

"Nice to meet you," said Jamie.

Coach Rudy proceeded to tell the children that Scurry had an extraordinary .48 goals against average as a senior the previous fall, in 1993. She made 124 saves and recorded a school-record 15 shutouts.

And he told them that, when Scurry was at UMass, the Minutewomen made it to the NCAA women's soccer tournament three times, including the Final Four.

"Did she wear the same pair of goalie gloves her whole college career?" asked Juanito.

"I never really noticed," said her coach. "I don't think it would have mattered what she wore on her hands, though. I think she could have worn oven mitts and made all those saves."

The kids looked discouraged.

"Yeah, she's something special," Coach Rudy said. "She's not done playing soccer yet. You'll see more of her, I'm sure."

The kids waved goodbye to the Minutewomen and made their way back to the locker.

6
THE ROSE BOWL

According to the Coach during their next journey through time and space, the U.S. women's soccer team won the gold medal at the 1994 Olympics in Atlanta, Georgia. In doing so, Briana Scurry and her teammates made the American public aware of women's soccer. In the 1999 World Cup, they wanted to make them fans.

A lot of the pressure to accomplish that feat was on Scurry's shoulders. By '99, she was considered the best goalkeeper in the world—and the No. 1 big-game keeper in the history of women's soccer. Her skills were unmatched by any female goalkeeper anywhere else on the globe.

But she didn't have her favorite gloves!

As Jamie, MJ, and Juanito peered out of the locker, they saw that they were once again inside a locker room. But which one, they wondered?

Their magic locker blended in perfectly, so it didn't take them long to find out. On the wall around the corner was a sign saying "Welcome U.S. women soccer players to Pasadena and the world-famous Rose Bowl." Underneath was the date: July 10, 1999.

"We must be at the finals," said Jamie, glancing around what appeared to be an empty room. "And the teams must already be on the field."

"How are we going to get on the field this time?" asked Juanito. "I don't see any press passes lying around."

"But there are three warm-up jackets and pairs of shorts, in kids sizes, in the locker," said MJ. "I wonder what they're for."

"They're for you guys to change into," said a woman's voice. "C'mon, you're late. The other honorary ball boys and girls are already on the field."

After dressing, the kids followed the stadium official out of the locker room and down to the field. As they walked, they asked her about the U.S. women's recent run.

The official told them that, since Chicago and the blowout of Nigeria, the Americans had defeated North Korea, 3-0, in Foxborough, Massachusetts. Then, they beat Germany, 3-2, in Landover, Maryland. Finally, they knocked off Brazil, 2-0, in Palo Alto, California.

The kids couldn't believe it. Even without her favorite goalkeeper gloves, Briana Scurry had held a tough German team to only two goals. Many experts had picked Germany to win the whole thing! She also earned two additional shutouts, one against the talented Brazilians. In that game, she made six saves, grabbing crosses out of the air and tipping shots over the crossbar.

The official got excited when she began describing just how phenomenal "The Rock" was against Brazil. She told the kids how Brazilian star Nene fired a bullet toward the U.S. goal from 35 yards out to start the second half. She described how Scurry saw the twisting shot the whole way. Taking a few steps back, Briana jumped as high as she could and punched at the ball. She made contact and deflected it up, where it hit the crossbar and flew over the goal.

Ten minutes later, she did it again. This time, only 12 yards out, Nene fired another shot toward the left corner. But once again, Scurry read it perfectly. She launched herself into the air just as Nene's foot struck the ball. Scurry got her hand on the shot just in time to knock it wide. The save protected the Americans' 1-0 lead.

After a few minutes, Jamie and the boys reached the field. As they walked out into the 90-degree Southern California heat, they couldn't believe their good fortune. They were on the same field that would be the focus of 90,000 screaming fan. Even the president of the United States was there! Another 40 million viewers would watch the game on TV in the United States. And another billion people would be sitting on the edges of couches around the world. No American network television audience that big had ever tuned in to watch a soccer game. Even more amazing was the fact that no women's sporting event had ever been seen by so many people, both in person or on TV.

"You guys must be my biggest fans," said Scurry, recognizing them on the sidelines as she warmed up. "Any luck finding my gloves?"

"No," said Jamie.

"I sure wish you had, because I could really use them today. China just defeated Norway, 5-0, and they pose a lot of problems for us."

"Why's that?" asked MJ.

"Well, they play a style very similar to ours," said Scurry. "Plus, their forward, Sun Wen, is the leading scorer in the tournament. And their keeper, Gao Hong, has given up the fewest goals."

"Even fewer than you?" asked Juanito.

"Yup," said Briana, her voice indicating just how upset she was. "She's been lights out."

It was then that a light bulb went off above the three time travelers' heads—at the same time. They looked at each other, then gave Scurry a reassuring look.

"You know, Briana," said MJ. "We've learned something while trying to find your lucky gloves."

"What's that?" asked Scurry.

"You don't need them," Juanito said. "It's not the gloves. It's *you*."

"But they're my lucky gloves, and this is the World Cup final," she said. "I can't afford to *not* be at my best. Not now. Not when the whole planet is watching."

"But you *are* the best," said Jamie, her friends nodding alongside her. "And you don't need a pair of goalie gloves to prove it."

"The Rock" looked long and hard at the three

youngsters in front of her. Finally, she nodded, too.

"You know, you're right," said Scurry. "I don't need a pair of gloves to help me do what I do. It's up to me and me alone. Thanks for helping me realize it."

As Scurry ran off to join her teammates, Jamie said, "I'm sure we just did what we came here to do."

"What you came here to do is stand over there with the rest of the children," said the lady official, who had overhead them talking. "Now, get moving. The game is about to start."

7
THE SAVE

The Americans came out on the attack, beating China to the ball. They wouldn't even let them past the center of the field.

But the Chinese adjusted. They began to drive back the U.S. Soon, the game was played entirely at midfield. Neither team had much in the way of a scoring opportunity. At the half, it was a scoreless tie.

Forty-five minutes of back-and-forth soccer later, it was still tied. The heat and humidity had obviously taken its toll. Players from both China and the United

States slumped to the ground, exhausted. But the game wasn't over. The teams were headed for overtime and the chance to score the one "golden goal" necessary for victory.

China had managed just two shots on goal during the game's first 90 minutes. But the Americans' defensive midfielder, Michelle Akers, had to leave due to injury. So the Chinese stepped it up a notch in the first 15 minutes of OT.

A few minutes into the extra period, China was awarded a corner kick. As the ball arched toward the goal, Scurry came off her line and went for it. But Chinese defender Fan Yunjie beat her to it. Her looping header sailed over Scurry's head and headed straight for the near post. Thankfully for the United States, Kristine Lilly was there to head the game-winner away.

The first 15 minutes of overtime ended with the score still knotted at 0-0. So did the second overtime period. The game would be decided on penalty kicks.

Jamie, MJ, and Juanito were sweating, and it wasn't

because of the heat. They were more nervous than they had ever been.

They watched as Briana Scurry prepared herself for the five Chinese players who would face off against her in the PK shootout. If she was nervous, it didn't show. Not even after China scored a pair of goals.

In fact, the shootout was tied at two goals when Chinese midfielder Liu Ying strutted toward the penalty box. The kids watched as Scurry swayed back and forth on the goal line. She was a picture of concentration.

Just as Liu approached the ball, Scurry sprang forward and flew to her left. She cut down the angle perfectly! As a result, she was able to deflect Liu's shot with ease. It was the biggest save of the Cup!

Lilly, Hamm, and Chastain then nailed their kicks. Once they did, the United States players went nuts. Chastain ripped off her shirt, waving it over her head to the roaring crowd. Scurry screamed and pumped her fist in the air.

It was the second time that a World Cup final at the Rose Bowl had ended on penalty kicks after a 0-0 tie. This was an entirely different game, though, than the 1994 men's final, in which Brazil beat Italy.

The main reason was that American fans had been cheering for their own team this time. They suffered through the heat with them, waiting for the one tiny advantage that would give their squad the victory.

Scurry gave the United States that advantage.

As the players celebrated on the field, Scurry ran over to hug her parents, brother, and friends. She stood there for a bit, watching her teammates. Then, she saw Jamie, MJ, and Juanito walking toward her. She made her way down out of the stands to greet them.

"Great game," said Juanito. "You were awesome!"

"Yeah," said MJ. "That was the best save I've ever seen."

Briana Scurry smiled.

After a few high fives, the kids said goodbye to Scurry, squeezed into the locker and took off.

"I wonder if we're on our way home," said Jamie. "You know, we did play two other sports in the back yard."

The locker stopped shaking and the glow of light coming through the air vents at the top disappeared. The door swung open.

"We're not home," said MJ, a smile forming at the corner of his mouth as he stepped outside into the sunlight. "I'm not sure, but I think we're in Africa."

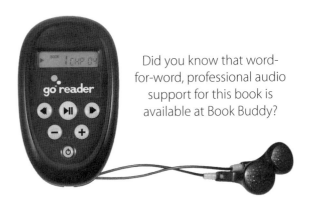

Did you know that word-for-word, professional audio support for this book is available at Book Buddy?

GoReader™ powered by Book Buddy is pre-loaded with word-for-word audio support to build strong readers and achieve Common Core standards.

The corresponding GoReader™ for this book can be found at: http://bookbuddyaudio.com

Or send an email to: info@bookbuddyaudio.com